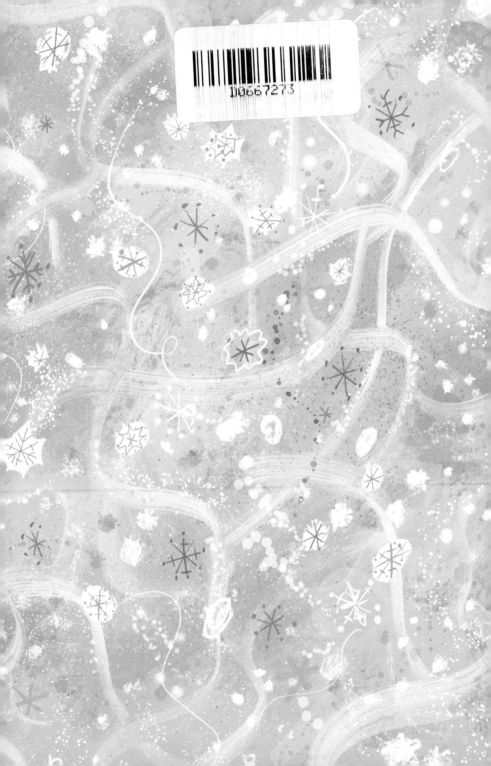

ZEKE THE WEATHER GEEK

THERE'S a LIZARD in My BLIZZARD!

For Cousin Caryl, who believed in
Zeke from the get-go — J.A-C.

For my uncle, Robert H. Gould,
who left me his nautical
barometer — A.M.

To my father, who was a
meteorologist at heart — P.J.B.

Acknowledgments:
We appreciate the expertise and
generosity of Steven Decker, PhD,
Associate Teaching Professor and
Director, Meteorology Undergraduate
Program, Rutgers University, and
Jason Shafer, PhD, Professor of
Atmospheric Sciences, Northern
Vermont University-Lyndon.

Text © 2023 Joan Axelrod-Contrada and Ann Malaspina
Illustrations © 2023 Paula J. Becker

Published in Canada and the U.S. by Kids Can Press Ltd.
25 Dockside Drive, Toronto, ON M5A 0B5

Kids Can Press is a Corus Entertainment Inc. company
www.kidscanpress.com

The artwork in this book was rendered digitally.
The text is set in Colby.

Edited by Debbie Rogosin
Designed by Barb Kelly

Printed and bound in Malaysia in 10/2022 by Times Offset
CM 23 0 9 8 7 6 5 4 3 2 1

MIX
Paper from
responsible sources
FSC® C001507

Library and Archives Canada Cataloguing in Publication

Title: There's a lizard in my blizzard / written by Joan Axelrod-Contrada and Ann Malaspina ;
illustrated by Paula Becker.
Names: Axelrod-Contrada, Joan, author. | Malaspina, Ann, 1957– author. | Becker, Paula, 1958–
illustrator.
Description: Series statement: Zeke the Weather Geek ; 1
Identifiers: Canadiana 20220231346 | ISBN 9781525304439 (hardcover)
Classification: LCC PZ7.A98 The 2023 | DDC j813/.6 — dc23

Kids Can Press gratefully acknowledges that the land on which our office is located is the
traditional territory of many nations, including the Mississaugas of the Credit, the Anishnabeg,
the Chippewa, the Haudenosaunee and the Wendat peoples, and is now home to many diverse
First Nations, Inuit and Métis peoples.

We thank the Government of Ontario, through Ontario Creates; the Ontario Arts Council; the
Canada Council for the Arts; and the Government of Canada for supporting our publishing activity.

ZEKE THE WEATHER GEEK

THERE'S a LIZARD in My BLIZZARD!

By Joan Axelrod-Contrada
and Ann Malaspina
Illustrated by Paula J. Becker

KIDS CAN PRESS

CONTENTS

1
Cloudy with a Chance of Flurries

Sunday afternoon

"Hey, Zeke, wait up!"

Zeke's little brother, Bub, was chasing him down Pine Street.

Clomp. Clomp. Clomp.

Bub stomped along the sidewalk in his dinosaur boots.

Zeke couldn't wait for Bub. He was tracking a snow cloud on Whirlwind, his weather scooter. The dark cloud was moving fast.

"I need to take a picture for the contest," Zeke shouted.

"A picture of what?" Bub shouted back.

"Winter! I'm going to get a picture of the first snowflake of the year!"

Bub asked too many questions. Six-year-old brothers never fail to annoy.

Zeke's curly red hair puffed out like a cloud. He liked having hair that told the weather. The wetter the air, the frizzier his hair.

"I want to see the snowflake, too!"

Why did Bub always have to do everything that Zeke did?

"Then hurry up!"

Clomp. Clomp. Clomp.

Bub's dinosaur boots were no match for a snow cloud.

The Winter Photo Contest happened every December in Miss Li's fourth-grade class. Zeke had wanted to win it ever

since first grade. His friends called him Zeke the Weather Geek. He was proud of that nickname. But what he really wanted was to be a Weather Warrior like his idol, WXYZ-TV Chief Meteorologist Freeze Jones.

Weather Warriors stay one step ahead of the weather. They're able to warn people about changes before they happen. They don't miss predicting a hard frost and letting the pumpkins die in the school garden, like he did. Zeke still felt terrible about that!

To prove he was a real Weather Warrior, Zeke needed an awesome photo of winter weather for the contest. Let the other kids take pictures of ski slopes or hot cocoa. He wanted his photo to show the awesomeness of a snowflake falling from the sky.

At the corner, Zeke braked for the red light. He checked the temperature on Thermo, the mini-thermometer dangling from his handlebars. Exactly 32 degrees Fahrenheit. Freezing point. Perfect for a snowflake.

Zeke's all-weather camera hung around his neck. Zeke liked to name his weather instruments. He called his camera Storm Shooter. Dad gave it to him before he left for Antarctica in September for the Polar Penguin Project. He was studying the effects of climate change on emperor penguins.

Clomp. Clomp. Clomp. Bub finally caught up with him.

"Don't you have to call Mom?" he asked.

Dad had given Zeke his old flip phone to call home so Mom wouldn't worry.

"Yeah, I better do that now."

Zeke punched in the number. When Mom answered, he told her they'd be home soon.

"Do you think Mom's really gonna get you a puppy?" Bub asked.

Today was Zeke's ninth birthday. All he wanted was a Saint Bernard puppy. He had already picked out its name. Blizzard.

"Of course. That's why, at breakfast, she said, 'Our family might be getting bigger!' I bet she's going to the pet store right now. She's picking out my Saint Bernard."

"Are you sure?"

"I'm sure," Zeke said. "Dad and I have been talking about it all year. Saint Bernards love snow, just like we do. Say you're trapped in a blizzard at the top of the Swiss Alps. A Saint Bernard would save your life."

"So would a dinosaur," said Bub.

Zeke tuned him out. Snow was coming, and Blizzard was waiting for him at home. His Mood Meter was rising. This birthday was going to be great!

Zeke carried his scooter with one hand and held Bub's elbow with the other as they crossed the street. Then the two boys headed up Summit Avenue to the highest point in the small city of Green River.

The snow cloud hovered overhead. Zeke looked up. No flakes yet.

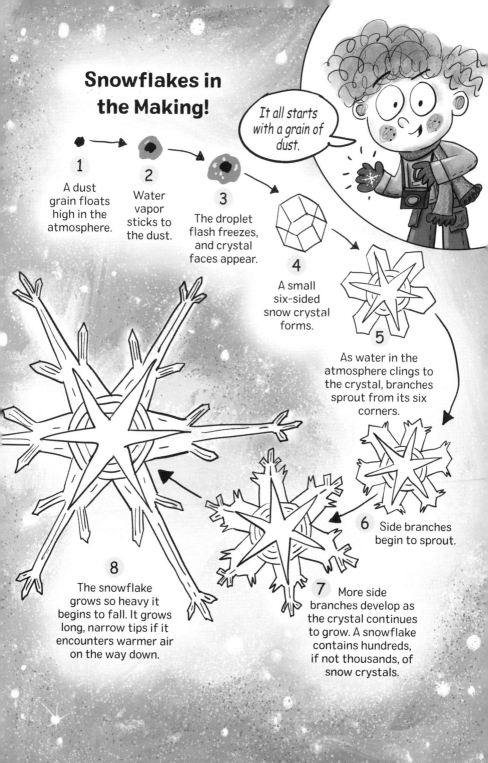

Snowflakes in the Making!

It all starts with a grain of dust.

1 A dust grain floats high in the atmosphere.

2 Water vapor sticks to the dust.

3 The droplet flash freezes, and crystal faces appear.

4 A small six-sided snow crystal forms.

5 As water in the atmosphere clings to the crystal, branches sprout from its six corners.

6 Side branches begin to sprout.

7 More side branches develop as the crystal continues to grow. A snowflake contains hundreds, if not thousands, of snow crystals.

8 The snowflake grows so heavy it begins to fall. It grows long, narrow tips if it encounters warmer air on the way down.

So Many Different Shapes!

❋ Because each snowflake encounters differences in temperature and humidity as it falls to the ground, no two flakes are alike.

❋ Low humidity gives rise to snowflakes with simple forms. High humidity makes for more intricate, lacy designs.

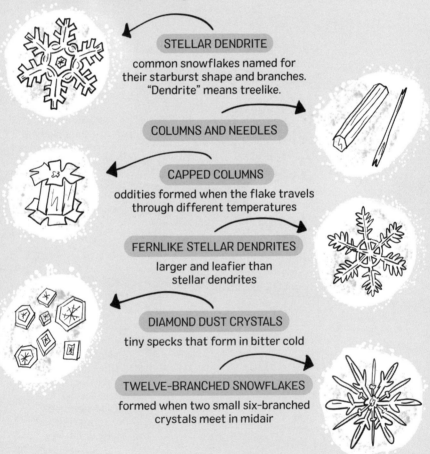

STELLAR DENDRITE

common snowflakes named for their starburst shape and branches. "Dendrite" means treelike.

COLUMNS AND NEEDLES

CAPPED COLUMNS

oddities formed when the flake travels through different temperatures

FERNLIKE STELLAR DENDRITES

larger and leafier than stellar dendrites

DIAMOND DUST CRYSTALS

tiny specks that form in bitter cold

TWELVE-BRANCHED SNOWFLAKES

formed when two small six-branched crystals meet in midair

Designer Snowflakes

* The saying "No two snowflakes are alike" is true in nature. But in the laboratory, it's a different story!

* Kenneth G. Libbrecht, a professor at the California Institute of Technology, has designed his own twin snowflakes. He's a scientist who studies the physics and beauty of snowflakes.

* The process isn't easy. Professor Libbrecht uses a chiller that recirculates air, several temperature controllers and a lot of special hardware.

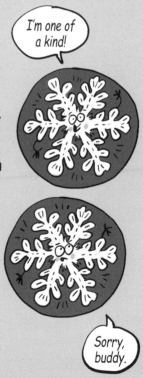

Clomp Clomp

2
Cold and Wet
Sunday around town

Luna Díaz lived at the top of Summit
Avenue in a tall house with purple shutters.
Who had purple shutters? Luna, of course.
She was the most annoying girl in Miss Li's
class.

Zeke tried to hurry past the house so
she wouldn't see him. But the front door
opened, and there she was. Zeke groaned.

"Hi, Zeke the Weather Geek!" she called.

Was Luna making fun of him? He could
never tell.

Zeke *did* like his nickname and tried to
live up to it. Sure, there was the pumpkin
disaster. But, last August, he had correctly
predicted the amount of rainfall during a
tropical storm. Seven inches!

At that moment, Mrs. Díaz stuck her head out the door. "Invite your friends inside, *mija*!"

Queen Violet winked at Zeke. Zeke shook his head. Weird!

"Sorry, Mrs. Díaz. We need to get home," he said. "Come on, Bub."

Zeke scootered down the other side of Summit Avenue. Bub clomped behind him.

"Did you see the ring around the moon last night?" Luna called.

Zeke didn't even look at the moon last night.

"The ring was from cirrus clouds," she screeched after them.

Why did Luna have to be so annoying? Zeke fumed. She was an astronomy geek. He wished she'd stick to outer space. Why did she have to know about clouds, too? What a show-off!

His scooter picked up speed. Bub tried to keep up.

Clomp-clomp. Clomp-clomp.

SPLAT!

An icy patch sent Bub flying. *Splat!* He landed on the sidewalk like an upside-down stegosaurus.

"Zeke!"

Bub was holding his leg. "My knee hurts," he whimpered.

Zeke sighed.

"Here, wear this," he said to Bub, handing him his helmet.

Zeke boosted Bub onto Whirlwind. They held the handlebars together, while Zeke walked beside the scooter and pushed.

The snow cloud would have to move on without him. He had to take Bub home.

As the sun began to set, the wind picked up. The last few blocks took forever. The city of Green River had a lot of hills. It wasn't easy to go up and down with Bub on his scooter.

As they turned up Pine Street, something wet and cold landed on Zeke's nose. A snowflake? Maybe he would get his winning picture after all!

Holding Storm Shooter steady, he tried to focus on the falling snow. But before he could snap a picture, rain began to hit his face.

Zeke wiped his eyes and checked Thermo: 34 degrees Fahrenheit. Above the freezing point. No snow would fall now. The whole trip had been a dud.

At least Zeke's new puppy would be waiting for him.

By the time the boys got to their little yellow house, it was almost dark and they were soaking wet.

Zeke burst through the door.

"Mom, we're home!"

But the house was quiet. Why didn't he hear Blizzard barking?

3

Home in the Rain

Sunday before supper

"Hey, birthday boy!"

Mom had been calling him that since Zeke woke up that morning.

"I hurt my knee!" Bub wailed.

Mom peeked out of her office. Her smile disappeared when she saw Bub's tears. She was wearing her Tech Lady hat and smock. Mom fixed people's computers, and her office was full of broken keyboards and mice that had stopped working.

Zeke looked around. No puppy. Maybe Mom was saving the surprise for later. She must have a good hiding spot. But wouldn't the puppy bark when he heard Zeke and Bub come in?

"Bub, what happened?"

"He slipped and fell," Zeke said. "Sidewalks ice up at 32 degrees."

Bub limped over to show her his knee.

"My poor Bubby."

She swept him into her arms. Mom had curly red hair like Zeke. But she used a special de-frizzing shampoo, so her hair couldn't tell the weather like Zeke's.

"You scraped your knee," she said. "Let's get a bandage."

Sometimes Zeke wondered if Bub fell down on purpose, just to get one of his nifty-wifty dinosaur bandages.

While Mom helped Bub put on the bandage, Zeke turned on the six o'clock news on WXYZ-TV, with Chief Meteorologist Freeze Jones. Listening to his forecasts always made Zeke's Mood Meter shoot up 10 degrees. One day, he hoped to meet Freeze Jones in person.

Tonight, the meteorologist wore his special storm visor with the yellow lightning bolt.

"It's going to be a wacky weather week! Rain today. Flurries tonight. But the big news is the blizzard coming later this week. Winds from the northeast will really whip it up! It's going to be a doozy!"

A blizzard! Zeke loved winter storms.

But right now, he had to find his new pup. He turned off the TV.

Maybe Mom had hidden the Saint Bernard in the backyard? But when Zeke put on his poncho and went outside, all he found was the rain. Good thing he needed to check his weather station anyway.

The weather station was in a plastic crate on the picnic table. Dad helped Zeke set it up before he left for Antarctica. They had attached a thermometer at the back, to keep it out of the sun. In the middle was a barometer made from a mason jar. The rain and snow gauge sat outside the crate.

The weather station reminded him of Dad. Zeke really missed him.

Dad always called home on Sundays, and today was Zeke's birthday, so there were two reasons for him to call. Zeke couldn't wait to talk to him.

He brushed away the raindrops on his weather instruments. How would he ever get his winter photo with all this rain? Zeke's Mood Meter sank to negative 30.

Temperature: 34 degrees Fahrenheit
Barometric Pressure: Falling
Snow: 0 inches
Rain: 0.5 inches

He wrote all the numbers in Sky Tracker, his weather journal. He slipped it back in its waterproof plastic bag and put the bag in the pocket of his cargo pants.

Back inside, the search continued. Zeke peeked under the kitchen sink. In the stinky dirty clothes basket. In Bub's dinosaur trunk. No Blizzard.

Then he tiptoed into his parents' room. Dad's closet held only his summer clothes and suits. No Saint Bernard. Zeke peeked in Mom's walk-in closet, which, now that he thought about it, would be the perfect place to hide a puppy.

Zeke slid past the empty shoeboxes Mom saved for his weather projects.

No puppy.

"Honey, can you get Bub's slippers for him?" Mom called from the bathroom.

This was it! The puppy must be in the bedroom he shared with Bub.

Zeke raced up the stairs, his heart beating faster. He looked in the closet and then under the beds.

Nothing except Bub's stinky dinosaur socks.

Why didn't he hear any barking? Where was the puppy?

Zeke's Mood Meter sank another 10 degrees.

Mom and Bub were waiting at the foot of the stairs.

"Do you have my dino feet?" Bub squealed.

Zeke sighed. He found Bub's furry green slippers behind his statue of a brontosaurus.

Mom gave Zeke her what-a-good-big-brother-you-are smile. He wanted to ask Mom about the pup, but he knew he couldn't. You can't ask about a birthday present that's supposed to be a surprise.

Where else could he look? Zeke thought hard.

Maybe Mom was hiding the puppy in the bathroom. Zeke turned to check it out, but then he realized that if the pup were there, Bub would have yelled up to him when Mom was putting on his bandage.

Where was it? He was still racking his brain when the doorbell rang.

The puppy wasn't in the house. Maybe the pet store delivered.

Zeke crossed his fingers. He held his breath. He opened the front door with his right hand and reached for the puppy with his left.

31

Air Has Weight!

∗ Air has weight, just like you!

∗ Air pressure is the weight of the air in the atmosphere pressing down on the earth.

∗ The more air above you, the higher the air pressure will be. The less air above you, the lower the air pressure will be. So, in high altitudes like on mountaintops, the air pressure is lower.

32

Air on the Move

✱ Air masses are constantly moving in the atmosphere. Warm air rises, creating low air pressure. Cold air sinks, causing high air pressure.

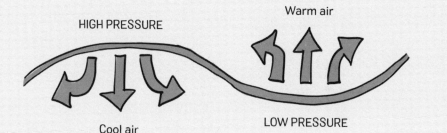

HIGH PRESSURE

Warm air

Cool air

LOW PRESSURE

✱ Rising and falling air pressure helps give us our weather.

✱ Low pressure is rising air, which helps form clouds. Expect stormy weather.

✱ High pressure generally means fair weather.

Yippee for low pressure! A storm is on the way!

33

Measuring Air Pressure

✳ Meteorologists use barometers to measure the air pressure. The word *barometer* comes from the Greek word *baros*, meaning weight.

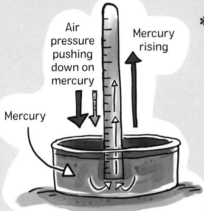

Air pressure pushing down on mercury

Mercury rising

Mercury

✳ A mercury barometer tracks air pressure using mercury in a glass tube. The mercury rises or falls depending on the air pressure surrounding the tube. This instrument looks like a thermometer.

✳ An aneroid barometer uses an airtight metal container that expands or contracts in response to the air pressure. A pointer moves as the air pressure changes. This instrument looks like a compass. The word *aneroid* means "without liquid."

✳ Digital barometers and apps for smartphones are new ways to measure air pressure.

Have Your Ears Ever Popped? Here's Why ...

✳ The higher you go above sea level, the thinner the air.

✳ Going down a mountain road or landing in an airplane, you may feel a change in air pressure.

✳ The air pressure pushing in on your eardrums is more than the pressure pushing out from the inside. This imbalance causes your ears to "pop." Swallowing or yawning helps get more air into your ears to bring them back to normal.

Birthday Washout

Sunday at supper

"Happy birthday to you!"

It was the singing pizza lady — and she was soaking wet.

No puppy. Zeke exhaled his disappointment in a breath big enough to blow out a forest fire.

"Are you going to let me in?"

The rain blew onto Zeke's face. He stepped back. The pizza lady sang the whole Pizza Pizzazz birthday song. Mom and Bub sang along. Every last verse.

Zeke had forgotten what a long song it was.

Finally, the pizza lady said goodbye, and Mom brought the box to the kitchen.

"I got your favorite! Hawaiian, with extra pineapple and cheese."

Zeke inhaled the delicious smell. "Thanks, Mom."

He really wished Dad were there. The birthday pizza wouldn't taste the same without him.

"First slice for the birthday boy."

Zeke gobbled up three slices of pizza in record time so he could get his birthday present.

Bub ate as slowly as a brontosaurus with a toothache. First, he chewed on one side of the slice. Then he gnawed on the other. He did the same thing with the next slice.

"Mom ..." Zeke tried to keep the whine out of his voice, but he failed miserably. He beseeched her with his eyebrows. "Please!"

"You'll have to wait," Mom said. "Your brother's still eating."

Bub took a long slurp of juice.

"Can't you hurry up?" asked Zeke.

"You can open your presents," said Bub, chewing slowly. "I can eat and watch."

Mom left the table.

She came back with a box in her hands.

"Ready?" she asked.

"Of course," Zeke said, staring at the box.

A puppy would never fit in something that small. But maybe it held a clue. A collar, or a rolled-up leash.

Instead of handing him the box, Mom put it on the table, removed the lid and lifted something out.

Zeke leaned in to see.

In her hands, she held the strangest, ugliest creature he had ever seen. It was the size of her hand, with bulging eyes and a tail as long as its body.

"A dinosaur!" Bub bounced up and down in his dino slippers, his mouth open and full of pizza.

Zeke couldn't believe his eyes. No soft fur to pet. No wet nose to nuzzle against his neck. No best friend to play with in the snow. This animal was not a Saint Bernard!

"It's called a bearded dragon. Don't you love her?" Mom stroked the scaly, spiny head. "I used to have a lizard just like her. I called her Lizzy."

"Can I hold her? Can I feed her? What should we name her?"

Mom shushed Bub. "That's up to Zeke. She's his lizard."

If only she had said his puppy. Zeke wondered why a spiny cold-blooded reptile even needed a name.

Mom turned to Zeke. "I know you want a dog, but a lizard can be a lot of fun, too. Give her a chance."

Zeke kicked the table leg. "Dad would have gotten me a Saint Bernard. And why hasn't he called yet?"

It was seven o'clock. Dad always called on Sundays at six thirty. And he wouldn't miss Zeke's birthday.

"In this family, we don't kick the table." Mom passed the lizard to Zeke. "Here, why don't you try holding her?"

Zeke felt the lizard's tiny feet on his palm. He wished they were a puppy's paws instead. Sharp lizard nails dug into his skin. "Ouch!"

"Bearded dragons need their claws to help them climb." Mom smiled and gave the lizard a pat. "I bought a tank for her. You and Bub can help me set it up."

"Great," Zeke said sarcastically.

Bub interrupted. "What does the dinosaur eat?"

"Lizards eat live crickets," she said. "Stan the Snake Man was all out of them yesterday. You boys will have to go to the pet store tomorrow."

A lizard? Live crickets? What next?

Mom brought out one more present. A handheld wind gauge from Grandma Willy. She knew he wanted to measure the wind speed. Grandma Willy always gave great presents. But the rest of Zeke's big day was a bust. He couldn't believe what a terrible birthday it had been.

No call from Dad.

Rain instead of snow.

And to top it all off, a lizard, not a puppy.

His Mood Meter dropped to negative 100 degrees.

Zeke Abramovich's ninth birthday was a total washout.

5
Below Freezing
Monday morning

By Monday morning, the rain had turned to flurries, just like Freeze Jones predicted. The snow was slowly piling up, but no blizzard yet. Zeke couldn't wait. He had missed his chance to photograph the first snowflake for the Winter Photo Contest. The blizzard would give him lots of new photo ops.

Zeke came downstairs wearing his favorite snowflake T-shirt. He sat down and poured syrup on his French toast.

"How is the lizard today?" Mom asked.

Zeke shrugged. Bub plopped into his chair. "She's great! I love her so much!"

Zeke didn't want to talk about the lizard. He got up from the table.

"Where are you going? You need to finish your breakfast," Mom said. "We're running late."

Zeke tuned her out. He had to check his weather station. Running out the back door, he felt snowflakes on his face. He pulled Sky Tracker out of his pocket and started reading his instruments.

Temperature: 31 degrees Fahrenheit

Below freezing.

Before Zeke could check the barometric pressure, Mom poked her head out the door.

"Zeke, the lizard needs fresh water!"

"Can't Bub do it?"

Bub had kept Zeke up all night, coochy-coochy-cooing with the lizard. Her tank was between their beds.

"No, sweetie, I asked you. It's your lizard," Mom said.

"Don't remind me," Zeke muttered under his breath.

He came inside, pounded up the stairs and changed the lizard's water.

After stomping back downstairs, Zeke gulped down the rest of his soggy French toast.

Mom put sandwiches in the boys' lunch bags and told them to hurry.

"But I have to finish filling out Sky Tracker!" Zeke said. With a blizzard on its way, he needed to record all the measurements. Those stats would help him track the storm. No more mess-ups like the pumpkin disaster.

"That can wait until you get home from school," Mom said.

"Dad wouldn't wait to record information about his penguins," Zeke said.

"Dad wouldn't want you to be late for school."

She gave Bub his dinosaur mittens and hurried them out the door.

Zeke and Bub were halfway down the block when Mom yelled after them, "Don't forget to stop at the pet store on the way home!"

Oh, yes. Zeke had to get creepy crickets to feed to his creepy lizard. Did he say HIS Lizard? Scratch that. THE Lizard.

By the time Zeke got to Room 22 with his late pass, Miss Li had already started class. She was wearing a red polka-dot dress. Miss Li wanted everything "on the dot" — like class starting on time.

Zeke's sneakers squeaked as he headed toward the window. That was the best place for a weather geek's desk. He could watch the weather all day long. Everyone's eyes were on him as he slid into his wobbly chair.

"Earth to Weather Satellite ... You're late!" Miss Li pointed at the clock. 9:07.

Weather Satellite. The class giggled. Some kids thought she was making fun of him. But Zeke knew she wasn't. Weather satellites were amazing. He wouldn't mind being a weather satellite!

The loudest giggle came from Luna. Her desk was in front of Zeke's. He had to stare at her head all day long. Actually, her hair looked strange today. Was it … purple? Yes, it was definitely purple, like the shutters on her house and her boots.

The only person who didn't giggle was Kiho, Zeke's best friend. Kiho was from Uganda. He was a whiz at math and wanted to be an engineer. He and Zeke had sat next to each other since the first grade.

"Glad you're here," Kiho whispered. "How's your puppy?"

"It's a lizard."

"Huh?" Kiho's eyebrows shot up. "Oh ... cool."

"Lizards aren't cool. Puppies are cool."

"What's its name?"

Before Zeke could answer, Miss Li clapped her hands.

"Boys, please stop talking and take out your math homework."

Zeke dug in his backpack. Smelly gym socks. Half-eaten candy bar. Rotten banana. No math folder! His Mood Meter sank below freezing.

6
Dracula's Icicle
Monday at school

He must have left his math folder at home.
He felt Miss Li's eyes on him.

"You forgot your homework *again*?"

Zeke nodded. Miss Li shook her head.

"Move your chair and look on with Kiho
for now."

When Zeke scooted his chair over, the
wobbly leg tilted so far, he almost fell off.

Kiho squatted down to check it out.

"I'll fix it," he said.

Kiho bit down on his lip. He always did
that when he was about to tinker with
something. The latch to the class guinea
pig's cage. Zeke's scooter. Even Luna's cat
door. You name it, Kiho could fix it.

Kiho pulled a dime from his front pocket. He used it like a screwdriver to tighten the screw on Zeke's chair leg.

"Thanks." Zeke wiggled to check it out. "Much better."

Kiho gave him the thumbs-up and sat back down.

Miss Li clapped her hands. "Before we start, I want to remind everyone about the Winter Photo Contest deadline on Friday. Last year, I had some students who turned in their photos late and couldn't be counted. Don't let that happen to you!"

"I won't be late!" said Luna. "I already took my photograph."

Of course she had.

"Well, that's excellent, Luna." Miss Li beamed her brightest smile. "It's always good to get things done ahead of time. What is it, if I might ask?"

"A picture of the first snowflake of the year. I snapped it just before the snow turned to rain yesterday."

Zeke almost fell off his chair. "She stole my idea!" he whispered to Kiho.

Luna turned around and glared. "I did not! It was my idea."

"Quiet, class!" Miss Li peered over her glasses. "Any questions about the contest?"

Simon's hand shot up.

"Do we have to write something about our photo?"

"Yes, a short caption," Miss Li answered.

Luna sat up straight in her chair. "I already wrote my caption. It's like a one-sentence ad for your photo."

Miss Li nodded. "Excellent, Luna."

Zeke groaned to himself. He looked out the window so he didn't have to see Luna's annoying purple hair. Outside, the snow had turned to freezing rain.

That's when Zeke saw it. A pointy icicle hanging from the maple tree next to the window. An icicle shaped like one of Dracula's fangs! It must have formed overnight after the snow changed to rain and then froze.

It was a dream come true. Luna's little snowflake couldn't beat a photo of this icicle. No way.

Zeke wanted to fly out the window and snap a photo right that minute. But there were hours to go before school was over, and he couldn't even do it then. He had promised Mom that he and Bub would go straight to the pet store for the lizard's food. "No detours," she had told them.

The lizard was ruining Zeke's life.

Click! The Snowflake Photographer

Wilson "Snowflake" Bentley was born in 1865 and grew up in Vermont, where the harsh winters gave him a lifelong fascination with snow.

For his fifteenth birthday, he got a microscope and began studying snowflakes.

He used a feather to carefully place each snowflake under the microscope.

But before he could draw what he saw, the snowflakes melted!

Snowflake Bentley talked his father into getting him a camera.

After much trial and error, he captured his first photographic image of a snowflake in 1885. He never gave up!

He took more than 5000 photographs of snowflakes and discovered that no two are alike.

Humid Like a Rainforest
Monday after school

The sign on the store said *Stan the Snake Man's Amazing Pet Store!* A giant rainbow-colored parrot was perched in the window. Before they went inside, Zeke called Mom to tell her they'd arrived. Once Bub opened the door, Zeke smelled bird doo and hamster droppings. The air in the store was as hot and humid as a rainforest.

It must be 99 percent humidity in here, Zeke thought. He started to sweat. His hair was turning as frizzy as Mom's barrel cactus plant. He had to get out of there! But before he could escape, Zeke heard a deep voice.

"Hi, I'm Stan the Snake Man! How can I help you?"

A man was kneeling on the floor. He wore a Hawaiian shirt and shorts.

"I'm Bub the Dinosaur Boy!" Bub said. "This is my brother, Zeke."

Stan the Snake Man stood up. He was wrapping something around his neck. It was a snake! The snake slithered around his shoulders. Its skin was the same color as the yellow flowers on Stan's shirt.

"Bub and Zeke. I know you! I hear you're a weather geek, Zeke. And you, Bub, are a dinosaur expert. Your mom bought our best beardie. What did you name her?"

Zeke shrugged. Why did everyone think a lizard needed a name? Dogs need names; lizards don't.

Bub started asking about the snake. Stan said it was a ghost ball python. "We call her Sweetie Pie." He looked into the snake's eyes like she was his best friend.

Stan and Bub talked a mile a minute.

Zeke saw the sign for dog supplies in the next aisle. It would be so much more fun to be buying bones and toys for a Saint Bernard!

Suddenly the glare coming through the store window caught his eye. He couldn't believe it. The sun had come out! What if the icicle melted before he got his winning shot?

"We need to buy crickets," Zeke said. "And we're kind of in a hurry."

"Sorry, boys," Stan said. "I have bad news. We didn't get our cricket shipment. It's been too cold. But I'm switching to a new company that ships them in heated containers. They should be here by the end of the week."

Bub was about to cry. "But I told the lizard that we're getting her crickets!"

As if the lizard understood English!

Stan the Snake Man calmed him down. "Don't worry, Bub. Your beardie will be fine eating greens for a few days."

"Greens?" Sweat dripped down Zeke's neck from the humidity. "Like salad greens?"

"Yes. Beardies particularly like arugula."

Mom always bought spring greens for salads. Stan said those should be fine.

"Let's go, Bub. I need to get you home and let Mom know I have an important photo to shoot."

But Stan was still talking — about the lizard, of course.

"Don't forget to turn on the heat lamps. Lizards need warm tanks. They should be 90 to 100 degrees at least."

He and the lizard weren't going to get along. Zeke didn't like hot, stinky pet stores or warm lizard tanks. He was a cold-weather guy, like Dad.

"Come on, Bub!" Zeke needed to get his shot of the icicle before it melted. It would be a great photo. A winner!

Stan the Snake Man's voice jolted him out of his thoughts.

"Have you looked into your bearded dragon's eyes?"

Why would Zeke want to do that?

Stan looked him straight in the eye. "Once you do, you'll know how special she is."

Special? A Saint Bernard puppy was special. A lizard was ... a lizard.

"Sorry." Zeke couldn't wait another second. The icicle would be gone! "We really have to go."

He pulled Bub outside.

But Stan had one more thing to say. "Get the lizard used to you now," he called. "It will really pay off. I promise!"

Zeke had no idea what Stan the Snake Man was talking about.

All Wet!

Precipitation is liquid or frozen water that falls from the sky down to Earth.

✴ Ever wonder why it never rains, snows or sleets when the sky is blue and clear? That's because precipitation comes from clouds.

✴ Precipitation is part of the water cycle.

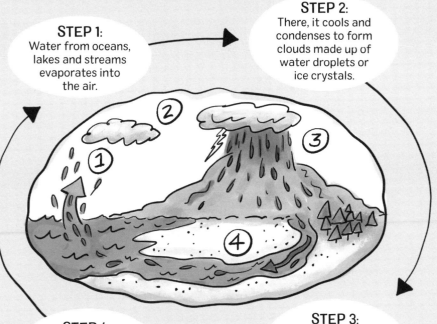

STEP 1:
Water from oceans, lakes and streams evaporates into the air.

STEP 2:
There, it cools and condenses to form clouds made up of water droplets or ice crystals.

STEP 3:
When the water droplets or ice crystals get too heavy, they fall as rain, sleet, hail or snow.

STEP 4:
The water falling on land collects again in oceans, lakes and streams.

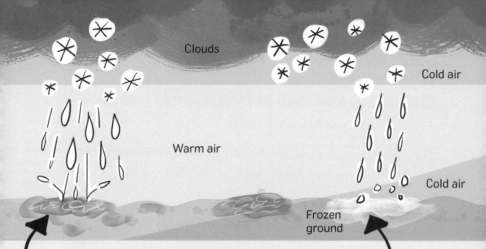

Clouds

Cold air

Warm air

Cold air

Frozen
ground

Winter Precipitation

Rain

* Believe it or not, most rain starts out high in the clouds as snow!

* Snowflakes melt when they fall through warmer air.

* If the air at ground level is also warm, the water droplets fall to Earth as rain.

Freezing Rain

* Freezing rain begins as snow, which melts when it falls through a layer of warm air.

* Near the ground, the water droplets fall through a thin layer of freezing air and cool down.

* If the ground temperature is below freezing, when the water droplets hit the ground they freeze and become freezing rain.

* Watch out for icy roads and sidewalks!

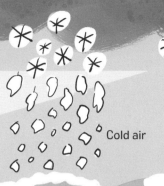

Cold air

Do you know the difference between frost and snow?

Meteorologist ZEKE

Sleet

* Sleet begins as snow, which then melts when it falls through a band of warmer air. Then the water droplets reach colder air and freeze. Tiny ice pellets form.

Snow

* Snow requires a column of cold air from the sky to the ground.
* Without the column of cold air, snow crystals can turn to freezing rain or sleet.
* Find out more about snowflakes on page 13.

Almost, But Not Quite

Dew and frost are wet like rain and snow, but they aren't forms of precipitation because they don't fall from the sky. Instead, they form from moisture in the air at ground level that condenses on surfaces.

8

Melting Point
Later Monday afternoon

Vroom! Zeke skidded into the school parking lot on Whirlwind. The air felt warmer. He hoped the icicle hadn't melted yet.

Kiho was waiting for him. He had his camera, too. In the shadow of the school, they checked Thermo for the temperature. It was 35 degrees Fahrenheit.

"1.7 Celsius," Kiho said.

Was he a math whiz, or what? Kiho could convert Fahrenheit into Celsius temperatures in his head in under five seconds!

"Did you know Uganda's average high temperature in December is around 79 degrees Fahrenheit ...?" Zeke began.

"And it rarely gets below 65," finished Kiho.

"The equator runs through Uganda. You never need a wool hat!"

Kiho always wore his wool hat in the winter, unlike Zeke, who let his curly red hair go free so it could tell the weather.

"Oh, I almost forgot." Kiho pulled a package out of his backpack.

"Happy birthday!"

Zeke ripped open the wrapping paper.

"A rooster weather vane! Now I'll know what direction the wind is blowing. Thanks for making it for me."

Kiho was always making useful gadgets for people.

Zeke held the weather vane above his head. The rooster's beak pointed northeast. Freeze Jones predicted the storm would come from that direction. The blizzard could be on its way!

"So, where's the famous icicle?" Kiho asked.

Zeke steered Whirlwind to the playground. Kiho speed-walked next to him. Zeke felt the sun on his shoulders.

"There it is!" Zeke shouted.

The icicle glittered like a diamond in the sunlight.

"That's an awesome icicle!" Kiho said. "It looks just like one of Dracula's fangs."

"That's exactly what I thought, too." Zeke focused Storm Shooter on the icicle.

"Wait! What's that sound?" asked Kiho.

"What sound?"

73

"That sound!"

Zeke heard it, too. *Drip. Drip. Drip.* The icicle was starting to melt.

He was about to snap a picture when ...

B O O o o m !!

The icicle was on the ground. Shattered in a million pieces.

Zeke's Mood Meter dropped to negative 30. First, he missed the first snowflake. Now, he missed the icicle. He kicked the broken ice. His chance at a winning photograph was fading fast.

In the sun, Thermo still read 35 degrees. Still above freezing. Just warm enough to wreck an icicle.

Kiho put his arm around Zeke's shoulders. "Don't worry, you'll find another one. You're Zeke the Weather Geek."

No, he wouldn't. Not with weather like this.

"Does that look like a polar bear's head?"

asked Kiho, pointing at a chunk of snow at the top of the slide. "Maybe it could be my winter photo."

Zeke had forgotten he wasn't the only one who still needed a photo. He stared at the snow chunk. "No. It looks like a blob."

"You're right," Kiho said. "Rats!"

Zeke tried snapping a photo of a slush puddle. Another dud.

"Zeke Abramovich. Too bad you didn't get the icicle before it crashed."

Luna always showed up at Zeke's worst moments. She wore purple snow boots and carried Queen Violet wrapped in a purple blanket. Too much purple!

"Did you guys know NASA found water on the moon?"

Zeke's ears perked up, but he pretended not to hear.

Kiho grabbed his arm. "I have another idea," he whispered.

Zeke jumped on Whirlwind. He didn't push off as hard as usual so that Kiho could lead the way. Luna tagged along. Ten minutes later, they were at the city garage, where a big truck was being loaded with salt. The mountain of salt was bigger than Mount Everest.

Kiho said, "You go for it, bro."

"Thanks."

He raised Storm Shooter again. This could be the winner!

Click. Click. Click.

Just then, Simon, their classmate, pulled up on his bike. He had a fancy camera on a strap around his neck. "What are you guys doing? I already took a photo of the truck. It's awesome!"

Another failed chance at winning the contest! Zeke lowered Storm Shooter.

"Time is ticking away," Luna said.

As if he didn't know that already. Leave it to Luna to make him feel worse.

Kiho turned to Luna. "Don't you have somewhere to be?"

"As a matter of fact, I do," said Luna. "I've got to set up my telescope. If there are no clouds tonight, I'll be able to see Mars."

Luna was always staying up late with her telescope. She wanted to be an astronaut, like Sally Ride.

As Luna walked away, Queen Violet peered back at Zeke. He shivered. The cat gave him the creeps.

"Do cats eat lizards?" Zeke asked Kiho on the way home.

"Probably," Kiho said.

"Good thing we don't have a cat. Bub's crazy about the lizard."

Kiho waved goodbye, and Zeke headed home.

After dinner that night, Zeke went upstairs to do his homework. But Bub was cooing to the lizard again, making it hard to concentrate. Zeke was glad when he heard Mom call to him from downstairs.

"You got an email!" she said.

"Who's it from?"

"Come read it."

Zeke flew downstairs to the family computer in the dining room. It was from Dad!

Hey Kiddo,

Happy birthday! Sorry I couldn't call yesterday. I dropped my satellite phone in a puddle while I was chasing a baby penguin to tag it. How's the weather in Green River? The weather here is warmer than ever. Climate change is real! Protect the penguins!

Love, Dad

Zeke had so much to tell, he didn't know where to begin.

Hi Dad, I didn't get a Saint Bernard for my birthday. Instead, Mom bought me a lizard that Bub loves. I don't. I miss you a lot. Love, Zeke

Dad wrote right back.

I didn't like Antarctica at first, but I'm starting to like it. Give the lizard a chance.

Dad signed off before Zeke could reply.

He hadn't even gotten to mention the photo contest. Zeke trudged back upstairs to his bedroom. Too bad there wasn't a puppy waiting for him instead of a lizard.

9

Winds Pick Up

Tuesday morning

"You look just like a dinosaur!"

Bub was talking to the lizard again.

Zeke had helped Bub feed the lizard last night. But he wasn't about to talk to her. Especially not at seven o'clock in the morning.

"I need my sleep!" he grumbled. But it was time to get up.

In the bathroom mirror, Zeke stared at his frizzy hair. It must be humid. Out the window, he saw a few snowflakes.

He got dressed and dashed to his weather station to record the measurements.

Temperature: 32 degrees Fahrenheit

Barometric Pressure: Falling

Snow: Not enough to measure

He attached Kiho's rooster weather vane to his weather station. The clamp made it easy. Kiho thought of everything.

Wind Direction: Northeast

Then he pulled Grandma Willy's wind gauge out of his pocket. The wind was picking up.

Wind speed: 10 miles per hour

He wrote down the measurements in Sky Tracker. The signs for a blizzard were all there. Increasing wind speed. High humidity. Cold ground temperature.

Zeke's Mood Meter was rising like the wind speed.

Date: Tuesday, December 4
Temperature: 32 degrees Fahrenheit
Barometric Pressure: Falling
Snow: Not enough to measure
Wind Direction: Northeast
Wind Speed: 10 miles per hour

The signs are there!
Here's hoping the blizzard is on its way!

At school, Miss Li was wearing her black and red polka-dot dress. That meant it was a test day. Zeke's stomach felt queasy. His Mood Meter plunged 20 degrees.

"Math test this afternoon," Kiho whispered. "Did you forget?"

Zeke didn't forget. He just didn't remember. He had other stuff to worry about. Lizards. Winter photographs. Dad. A weather geek could only think about so much!

The morning went quickly. Zeke was too hungry at lunch to study. At recess, he and Kiho joined the other boys in a game of tag. He forgot all about the test.

When Miss Li handed it out, and Zeke read the first question, he knew he was in trouble. His mind was as blank as a snowdrift. He should have studied.

He looked out the window. A patch of blue sky hung over the playground. If he were Miss Li, he'd give math tests on boring-weather days.

Not when a blizzard was coming. Watching for a big storm made it too hard for Zeke to concentrate!

"Earth to Weather Satellite!" Miss Li said. "Let's focus on math. The clock is ticking."

Zeke answered a few problems but got stuck again. None of the numbers made sense. In front of him, Luna jotted down her answers quickly. Kiho was already done.

All Zeke could think about was watching Freeze Jones tonight on the news. He wondered whether or not they'd get the big blizzard.

Miss Li's voice broke into his thoughts. "Finish up, class! You have one more minute before I collect your papers."

One more minute would not help him finish the test. Zeke snuck another peek out the window. The tree branches were swaying. Higher winds meant the blizzard was getting closer.

Miss Li collected the tests. Zeke wasn't even close to finishing. His Mood Meter sank.

Finally, the end-of-school bell rang. *Brrring!*

Zeke and Kiho put on their jackets and boots, and rushed out the door. Luna put on her purple boots and followed the boys to Whirlwind. For once, Bub wasn't tagging along. He was going to a playdate with a friend.

"Can I walk home with you?" Luna asked. "My house is on the way."

Zeke studied her face. No Luna Díaz I'm-the-best smirk. Just a regular smile. Still, he wasn't sure what she was thinking.

"I heard you yesterday," she said. "I didn't steal your snowflake idea. I got it from the internet."

Zeke shrugged. He didn't know if he believed her or not.

Luna clutched her heart. "I promise on my cat's blue eyes ... I'm no thief."

Both boys groaned, but they made room for her on the sidewalk.

Zeke unlocked Whirlwind and pushed off. Kiho and Luna jogged next to him. He stopped to take a picture of the swaying trees along the way. *Click.*

"It's getting too windy," said Luna, holding on to her purple hat.

"Yeah, I'm freezing," Kiho said. "Let's all go home."

Before he turned to go, Zeke took a quick look at the photo.

A blur. His Mood Meter plunged to negative 50. The contest was just three days away. And Zeke needed a whopper of a photo. The blizzard had better hurry up.

Blizzard!

The U.S. National Weather Service defines a blizzard as a severe winter storm that combines the following conditions for at least three hours:

* Strong winds, or frequent gusts of wind, of 35 miles (56 km) per hour or higher

* Falling or blowing snow

* Reduced visibility that makes it hard for a person to see farther than a quarter of a mile (0.4 km)

Cold temperatures and heavy snowfall are common, but not required, for a blizzard.

Get ready for some wild and wacky weather!

How a Blizzard Forms

Cold, dry air

Blizzard area

Warm, moist air

Strong winds

* Blizzards can occur when warm, moist air collides with cold, dry air.
* The difference in temperatures causes strong winds.
* Cold air is heavy and dense, and pushes up the lighter, warm air.
* If there's enough moisture in the air, and the temperatures in the air and on the ground are both below freezing, snow will fall and a blizzard may result.

Blizzards Around the World

Blizzards occur in all parts of the globe, except around the equator. Different countries have different ways of determining when a snowstorm becomes a blizzard. For instance, Canada issues a Blizzard Warning for winds of 24.8 miles (40 km) per hour or greater. In Canada, a snowstorm has to last at least four hours to be called a blizzard.

The Schoolhouse Blizzard

On January 12, 1888, a huge blizzard struck the U.S. Upper Midwest.

The morning started out above freezing. But while children were in school, Arctic winds and snow blew in.

In some places, temperatures fell to –40˚F (–40˚C), and winds blew at almost 60 miles (97 km) per hour. It was a whiteout!

Children struggled to get home from school. In an amazing rescue, teacher Minnie Freeman led her students to shelter after the roof blew off her schoolhouse in Nebraska.

Others weren't so lucky. Between 250 and 500 people died.

Today, meteorologists have more tools to forecast dangerous blizzards like this one, so people can be prepared.

F = Fahrenheit · C = Celsius

Ground Blizzard

Some blizzards occur without any snow falling from the sky. Instead, snow already on the ground combines with strong winds to create blizzard conditions. Ground blizzards are common in Antarctica.

Snowdrifts

✷ Snowdrifts form when winds blow snow into mounds.

✷ On January 17, 2020, a powerful blizzard in Newfoundland buried highways in snowdrifts that were up to 15 feet (4.5 m) high.

✷ Snowdrifts from a blizzard on March 11–14, 1888, buried New York City streets under drifts 20 feet (6 m) high — as tall as a giraffe!

Whiteout!

✷ Watch out for whiteouts! They can be dangerous.

✷ Blowing snow and cloudy skies block and scatter the light, resulting in low visibility.

✷ Drivers can't see the road or the cars ahead of them. This leads to accidents.

✷ People on foot can get lost. In the Schoolhouse Blizzard of 1888, the storm was so blinding that farmers couldn't find their way from the barn to the house, even though they were just feet away.

Where are my mittens?

✷ In a whiteout, you may not be able to see your own boots!

10
Winter Storm Watch

Tuesday evening

The lizard grabbed a tiny bite of lettuce from Mom's hand.

Bub clapped. "Can I feed her now?"

"Of course you can!"

The lizard sat between them on the living room rug.

"She's eating my lettuce, too!" Bub squealed.

"Are you going to be done soon?" asked Zeke from the couch. "Freeze Jones's weather report is on in two minutes. I need quiet!"

The barometer at his weather station showed a drop in pressure that afternoon. Also, Zeke's sinuses were prickly. Two signs that the big storm could be getting closer.

"Don't you want to give it a try, Zeke?"
Mom asked.

Well, why not? The lizard wasn't a Saint
Bernard, but she did seem hungry. For a
second, Zeke forgot about the weather.
He knelt down and tried to feed the lizard.
She darted away, ignoring him. How rude! A
minute later, she climbed up Dad's handmade
coffee table. Its legs had rough wood for her
feet to grip.

Zeke reached for the remote. But then,
something strange happened. The lizard beat
him to it. She stepped on the easy-touch
PLAY button with her right front foot.

CLick!

The TV switched on, and the sound blasted. "Live from Green River, I'm Freeze Jones, and this is a special storm tracker report."

"Did you see that?" Bub shouted.

Mom's jaw dropped to the floor. "My Lizzy never turned on the TV."

Zeke was too shocked to speak. The lizard didn't move an inch. Her eyes stared straight at the TV. If she did that on purpose, she was pretty smart for a lizard. But it was probably an accident. Zeke still wasn't about to give her a name.

Freeze Jones spoke in his booming voice.
"The National Weather Service has issued
a Winter Storm Watch starting tonight.
That means conditions are favorable for a
blizzard. But, whether or not one develops,
we'll have to wait and see."

"Why are there still blizzards?" Bub asked.
"Isn't the world getting hotter?"

Zeke shook his head. "Climate change doesn't work that way. Because the oceans are warming up, more moisture is getting into the air, which makes for worse storms, even in winter. We could have more blizzards instead of fewer."

Mom and Zeke turned their attention back to the TV.

Freeze Jones whipped off his snowflake bow tie. He tacked it up on his weather map right over the small city of Green River. To the north was a big *C* for a cold front. To the south was a big *W* for a warm front.

"I predict that warm, moist air from the Atlantic Ocean will ride over cold air from Canada, making for blizzard conditions right here in our fair city." Freeze Jones pointed to Green River. "Within the next 48 hours, we could be seeing the blizzard of the decade. Be prepared for dangerous wind gusts and high snowdrifts."

Mom jumped up. "I'm going to check the storm windows. And I have to make sure we have enough food in the house, in case we're snowed in. I need to make a trip to the market."

"Don't forget the arugula!" Bub said.

On the TV, Freeze Jones waved his arms in the air. "Yes, yes, yes. Be prepared! Make sure you have enough batteries, candles, food and water, and pet supplies. Ladies and gentlemen, I stand by my prediction. It's going to be a whopper of a storm right here in Green River."

A whopper of a storm! Dad would love a blizzard. But Zeke hadn't heard from him since his email. And he still hadn't called. Mom said Zeke just had to be patient.

"Blizzards can be dangerous," she said now. "This time, I hope Freeze Jones is wrong."

Zeke didn't. A blizzard would be awesome. Giant drifts. Lots of photo possibilities. He'd finally get his prize-winning winter photo. Zeke's Mood Meter shot up for the first time since morning.

Dangerous Wind Gusts

Wednesday afternoon

At recess the next day, Zeke kept an eye on Thermo. He also checked Grandma Willy's wind gauge. He pulled Sky Tracker out of his cargo pants and scribbled some notes.

Temperature: 26 degrees Fahrenheit

Wind Speed: 15 miles per hour

Kiho was at the top of the climbing gym. Zeke scrambled up. Snow flurries had started that morning. Tiny flakes stung his face.

"Hey, you won't believe my weather readings," Zeke said. He showed them to Kiho, who agreed that the storm could be on its way.

Then Kiho reached into his pocket and handed Zeke a hook.

Zeke scratched his head. "It looks like a shower curtain hook."

Kiho the Fix-it Wizard smiled. "Yep, it's for hanging your new wind gauge."

"Thanks, dude. It looks like the blizzard is heading right for us."

"I heard it might head north of us," said Kiho.

"That's not what Freeze Jones said."

Luna was staring at Zeke and Kiho from the wooden bench. She probably thought they were having more fun than she was.

"Maybe you should take a picture of the wind!" she shouted. "That would be a winner!"

What she really meant was that you can't take a photo of the wind. It would be a real loser. Mom called that sarcasm, saying the opposite of what you meant. Zeke hated sarcasm. Luna wasn't usually sarcastic. Maybe having no friends was getting to her.

Kiho shrugged. "Don't even listen to her! You'll get a great photo. I know you will."

But Zeke was running out of time. The contest deadline was only two days away.

After recess, Miss Li was wearing her green polka-dot scarf. She always wore that scarf when she handed back tests.

"Most of you did pretty well," she said. "Some of you need to study harder."

Was she looking right at Zeke?

Miss Li walked around the room. Zeke didn't want to see his grade on the math test. He really didn't. Then the test was in his hands. F. His salami sandwich sank to the pit of his stomach.

"Weather Satellite, I know you can do better," said Miss Li. "I'd like you to stay after school to retake the test."

Was she kidding? The blizzard was coming. And Zeke had promised Mom that he and Bub would get the crickets after school. Stan the Snake Man might close early if the snow got too bad.

"The lizard needs supper!"

After Zeke told her about the crickets, Miss Li's face turned as green as her scarf. She must not like thinking about a lizard eating live crickets. Zeke didn't blame her.

She cleared her throat. "The test will take 30 minutes. I'm sure the crickets will still be there."

Zeke called Mom to let her know he'd be staying after school, so she could pick up Bub.

"Don't forget the crickets," Mom said.

He sighed. "Okay."

At two thirty, Zeke was stuck in his seat.

Kiho gave him a sad look, like he felt sorry for him. "Later, dude," he said.

Everyone but Zeke left to go home.

Miss Li let him practice first. When Zeke saw the test again, the problems looked a little easier. He got a B+ and a smiley face. "Zeke Abramovich, you're free to go," Miss Li said.

Outside, the flurries had changed to light snow. Tree branches whipped around in the wind. Zeke wanted Freeze Jones to be right about the blizzard. Freeze Jones was his hero. But predicting the weather is hard. Even the best meteorologist is wrong sometimes. Zeke tried not to hope too much.

The minute he got home, Bub rushed up to him.

"Where are the crickets?"

Zeke had totally forgotten.

He jumped back on Whirlwind. He didn't have much time. He had to get home before dark. That was one of Mom's rules.

The snow and wind picked up. By the time he got to the pet store, he could barely see six inches in front of him.

Gone home. You should, too! said the sign on the door.

Whoosh! A sharp gust from the northeast almost knocked him off the sidewalk. Winter storms were dangerous, just like Mom and Freeze Jones said.

Get Ready for a Blizzard!
Plan Ahead and Be Prepared

* Make a list of emergency phone numbers.

* Know where to get weather information.

* Charge phones and computers.

* Plan what to do in case you lose power.

* Put together an emergency weather kit.

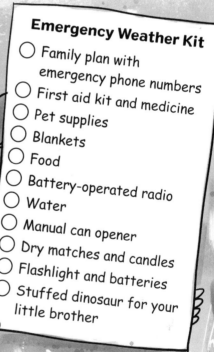

Emergency Weather Kit

○ Family plan with emergency phone numbers
○ First aid kit and medicine
○ Pet supplies
○ Blankets
○ Food
○ Battery-operated radio
○ Water
○ Manual can opener
○ Dry matches and candles
○ Flashlight and batteries
○ Stuffed dinosaur for your little brother

Stay Inside!

Going outside during a blizzard is dangerous. Our bodies lose heat when cold wind hits exposed skin. That wind makes the air feel colder than the actual temperature. This is called windchill. It can even cause frostbite. So be safe! Stay indoors.

Be a Good Neighbor

When a blizzard is on its way, be sure to check on your neighbors and relatives. They may need your help!

Blizzard Warning

Wednesday evening

Zeke had to climb Summit Avenue to get home from the pet store. On the sidewalk in front of Luna's house, his scooter hit an icy patch. He fell over and landed hard.

AAOOUU!

Was that Luna laughing at him? No, the purple shutters of her house were closed. The howling sound was the wind, which was getting stronger by the second.

Zeke was okay, but Thermo had broken in half. His Mood Meter plunged to negative 30. All he wanted was to get home. Whirlwind slid up and down Green River's famous hills.

Before he went inside the house, Zeke wiped the snow off Whirlwind. He put the scooter in the shed. Bub swung open the kitchen door.

"You DON'T have the crickets? She's going to starve to death!"

"No, she's not," Mom called from her office. "She'll be fine with the greens."

"But I want her to have crickets," Bub whined.

It all sounded like *bla-bla-bladee-bla* to Zeke. He rushed back outside to his weather station.

Temperature: 17 degrees Fahrenheit

Barometric Pressure: Falling superfast

Snow: 2 inches

Wind Speed: 23 miles per hour

Wind Direction: Northeast

If the wind speed reached 35 miles per hour, the storm would officially be a blizzard — and Freeze Jones would be right again. Zeke graphed his findings in Sky Tracker.

The pattern confirmed the blizzard was on its way.

He raced back inside. Zeke couldn't wait to hear Freeze Jones's weather report.

Bub was in the living room with the lizard. "Are you a good girl, T-Rex?" he cooed.

"That's a dinosaur's name, not a lizard's!" Zeke rolled his eyes.

Bub shoved his hands on his hips. "Well, if you'd give her a name, then I wouldn't have to call her T-Rex!"

"Boys! Please!" Mom called from her office.

"Sorry," they said at the same time.

They turned to face the lizard. Fast as lightning, she climbed up the coffee table. Then she pressed the easy-touch PLAY button.

"She did it again!" screeched Bub.

Zeke's mouth fell open. So, it wasn't an accident. Who knew a lizard could be so smart? A Saint Bernard would probably just chew the remote.

"Live from Green River, this is Freeze Jones with a special storm tracker report."

Freeze Jones wore his blizzard sweater and snowflake visor. He waved his arms wildly in front of the big *C* for cold front on the weather map.

"The National Weather Service has upgraded its Winter Storm Watch to a Blizzard Warning. The following conditions are expected in 12 to 18 hours: blowing snow reducing visibility to one-quarter of a mile or less for three hours or longer, and sustained winds of 35 miles per hour or frequent gusts to 35 miles per hour or greater."

He took a deep breath. "All of you folks get ready to hunker down with your cocoa. It's going to be a wild ride."

He unclipped his bow tie and reached over to the weather map.

"Oh, no," Bub said. "He's putting his bow tie on Green River."

A smile spread across Zeke's face. "That means the blizzard is going to hit us straight on."

Freeze Jones took off his glasses. "The next 12 hours are critical. The air pressure has been dropping fast for 24 hours. Conditions are extremely dangerous. We call this a bomb cyclone."

"A bomb cyclone!" Zeke pumped his fist in the air.

"Wow," said Mom, who held a broken laptop in her arms. "I hope the power doesn't go out."

Once again, Freeze Jones pointed to his snowflake bow tie. "Ignore all the naysayers! Prepare yourself for the big blizzard right here in Green River."

Mom pulled nervously on her ear. "I miss your father."

"So do I," Bub said.

"Me too," said Zeke. Even though a blizzard was exciting, it would be more fun with Dad around.

Even the lizard looked like she wished Dad were home. Her head was resting on the coffee table. Dad would want to be here, too. A blizzard needed Weather Warriors — and Dad was definitely a Weather Warrior. For now, Zeke was on his own.

Whiteout
Thursday morning

"Snow day! Snow day!"

Bub's shrieks were like a car alarm going off. Zeke jumped out of bed and pulled back the curtains.

What a storm! Snowflakes shot sideways like tiny missiles. It was a total whiteout. Mrs. Gully's house next door had disappeared. The wind howled like a pack of wolves.

He grabbed Sky Tracker from his night table and got dressed. He needed to check his weather station and make sure everything was secure. What if Kiho's weather vane was spinning around like a carnival ride?

When Zeke got to the kitchen, Mom was blocking the back door. He tried to get around her.

"Don't even think about going outside!" She stretched out her arms like a giant snowbird.

Mom wore her fluffy earmuffs. She always wore earmuffs in snowstorms, even indoors.

"I need to check my weather instruments. Please?!" Zeke tried to look adorable like Bub. "This could be the blizzard of the decade!"

"That's exactly why we're staying inside today," said Mom, heading to the stove. "I'm making chocolate chip pancakes."

Zeke ran to turn on the TV. Freeze Jones was in the middle of an emergency storm report.

"I have a special message for all my viewers. We have hazardous conditions in Green River. It's dangerous outside. So everyone stay inside, snug as a —"

Suddenly the TV went dark. The cable was out. Now there would be no weather news at all.

Bub helped Mom crack the eggs. Zeke sat at the table. His knees jiggled. He needed to measure the snowfall. Check the wind speed. Record the temperature and the barometric pressure. Plus, he still needed his winter photo.

Zeke's Mood Meter was dropping fast.

Then he got a sweet whiff of butter and maple syrup. Zeke couldn't resist Mom's chocolate chip pancakes. He ate five big ones with a super lot of syrup. Bub gobbled down four.

"Are you sure I can't go outside?"

Mom shook her head. "You heard what Freeze Jones said. Please find something to keep your brother busy."

A blizzard in Green River, and Zeke was stuck inside! His Mood Meter sank to negative 100.

Zeke spent the day doing weather projects. First, he made Bub a dinosaur weather vane. Then he did the egg-in-the-bottle trick that shows the power of air pressure. Mom helped by lighting a piece of paper and dropping it in a glass bottle. As the air got hotter, the air pressure increased. Zeke placed a peeled hard-boiled egg on top of the bottle. "Wait a minute. Let the air in the bottle cool down."

Bub held his breath.

"When air in the bottle cools, the pressure drops," Zeke said. "Watch what happens next."

Pop! The higher air pressure outside pushed the egg into the bottle. "It's magic!" Bub squealed.

Zeke looked out the window at the whirling snow. A blizzard is also caused by a low pressure system clashing with a high pressure system. Cool!

Egg shells →

← Boiled Egg

After lunch, he helped Bub make a weather journal.

"It's time to feed the lizard," Mom said.

Zeke started to say, "Let Bub feed her."

Then he remembered Dad's advice. *Give the lizard a chance.*

"Okay, I'll do it."

Zeke grabbed a leaf of arugula from the refrigerator. Up in the bedroom, he leaned over her tank. The heat lamps were on. The cage was toasty warm. The lizard was sitting on a rock.

On a day like this, a Saint Bernard would be pulling people from snowdrifts. Bringing food to stranded travelers. Rescuing lost children.

"I bet you wish you were a Saint Bernard." Zeke whispered so no one could hear him talking to the lizard.

The lizard stretched her neck toward the lamp. Zeke dangled a piece of arugula near her mouth.

"I can't check my weather instruments during the blizzard of the decade," Zeke said a little louder. "What do you think of that?"

The lizard tipped her head up. Her tongue darted out and caught the arugula.

Chomp. Chomp. Chomp.

"I can't even go out to take my winter photograph — and the contest ends tomorrow!"

This reminded him of the frostbitten pumpkins. His Mood Meter fell again.

Zeke looked at the lizard. What did Stan the Snake Man say about her eyes? That Zeke had to look into them?

The lizard's golden eyes glittered.

Maybe Stan was right. They needed to get used to each other.

Zeke reached out his hand. The lizard's sharp claws tickled his palm. Looking at him, she chewed the arugula.

"Do you mean that I shouldn't give up?"

The lizard kept chewing. A gust of wind shook the house. *Crack!* A branch must have fallen nearby.

The furnace clunked loudly, and the lights went out.

If only he could zap them back on. But even Weather Warriors can't turn the power back on. Instead, he shivered in the darkness.

Climate Change

* Climate change is a change in average weather patterns over a long period of time.

* It is different from changes in weather. Weather is the day-to-day conditions in an area: temperature, wind and precipitation.

It's like Earth has a fever!

* Since 1880, when global temperatures began to be recorded, average temperatures have risen about 2 degrees Fahrenheit (1 degree Celsius).

* The gradual increase in the temperature of Earth's atmosphere is called global warming. It is part of climate change.

* Even when the global temperature rises, some places can still be very cold.

Effects of Climate Change

- Warming oceans
- Rising sea levels
- Melting glaciers
- Worsening wildfires
- Destruction of habitat
- Flooding
- Increased humidity
- More days with extreme heat
- Oceans becoming more acidic
- Increased air pollution
- More frequent and intense blizzards and other extreme weather

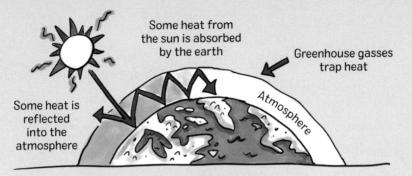

Some heat from the sun is absorbed by the earth

Greenhouse gasses trap heat

Some heat is reflected into the atmosphere

Atmosphere

The Greenhouse Effect

* Greenhouse gases play a big part in climate change.

* Like a greenhouse that stores heat to help plants grow, greenhouse gases trap heat in the atmosphere.

* Temperatures on Earth's surface start to rise. This is global warming.

* The two most harmful greenhouse gases are carbon dioxide and methane.

* Carbon dioxide (CO_2) makes up 82 percent of greenhouse gas emissions in the United States.

* Greenhouse gases get into the air when we burn fossil fuels like coal, natural gas and oil.

* Cars, trucks and planes, electric power plants and factories are some of the biggest sources of greenhouse gases.

* Earth needs to be warm for us to live, but not too warm. Even a small rise in temperature can cause many changes.

Fight Climate Change:
Walking to School and Other Things You Can Do!

* Turn down the heat. Wear a sweater instead.
* Ride a scooter, walk or use public transportation.
* Reduce trash by reusing and recycling.
* Eat less meat and dairy.
* Avoid items that you use once and throw away.
* Fly in airplanes less often.
* Tell your representative in government to support laws and policies that fight climate change.
* Plant a tree.

Hold on to Your Shirt!
Did you know that factories making new clothes produce a lot of CO_2? If you wear hand-me-downs and only get new clothes when you really need them, you can help reduce harmful greenhouse gas emissions.

14

Blizzard of the Decade

Thursday evening

"Is she dead?" Bub asked.

Mom shone her flashlight into the lizard tank. The three of them peered in. The lizard wasn't moving. She looked like she was stuck to her rock.

"Let's hope the power comes back on soon," Mom said. "Beardies don't like the cold."

Zeke remembered Stan at the pet shop telling him about this.

Something strange was happening. Zeke was worried about the lizard. Really worried! He had to do something.

Bub held the flashlight while Zeke reached inside the tank. Zeke felt the lizard's spiny body.

He gently cupped her in his hands and pulled her out.

Mom and Bub leaned over to look at her. "Is she breathing?" Bub's voice trembled.

Zeke's hands were freezing cold. They couldn't warm up the lizard.

Think quickly, Zeke told himself. Lizards are cold-blooded animals. They sense any change in air temperature.

The lizard's back was turning brown. Wow! She was a weather instrument like Zeke and his frizzy hair.

But lizards need warmth. Without heat, she could … Zeke didn't want to think about what could happen.

Then Zeke had an idea. He was wearing the Polar Penguin Project sweater Dad had sent him from Antarctica. He lifted up the front of the thermal fleece with his left hand. With his right hand, he put the lizard against his skin. He held her in place by his heart.

Since he wasn't sick, Zeke's body temperature was normal: 98.6 degrees Fahrenheit. That should be warm enough for the lizard.

Mom and Bub looked at him in surprise.

"I thought you didn't like the lizard," said Bub. "Now you're saving her life. You're like her sun!"

Weather Warrior to the rescue!

Mom gave Zeke a careful hug so as not to crush the lizard.

"Can you get Storm Shooter?" he asked Bub. He still needed that winter photo.

Click! Zeke looked at the selfie. Too bad it didn't have any snow in it.

Then they all went downstairs. Zeke kept his hand firmly on the lizard under his sweater. Outside, the snow was falling harder. The gale winds roared. The house shook. A terrible thought crossed his mind.

His weather station could blow away.

"What if — ?" he started to say.

Mom read his mind. "Don't worry about your weather station. There's nothing we can do right now," she said. And she was right.

At 5:55 p.m., a loud rumble shook the house.

"Help!" Bub shrieked. "There's a robber in the basement!"

It wasn't a robber. The furnace was working again. The electricity was back on.

Once the house warmed up, Zeke pulled the lizard out from under his sweater. He put her down on the coffee table. She made a beeline for the TV remote. Her right front foot landed on the easy-touch PLAY button. The cable worked!

"Live from Green River, I'm Freeze Jones, and this is the storm tracker news."

Zeke yelled, "The lizard did it again! She turned on the TV!" He gave her a little pat on the head.

Freeze Jones reported the latest snow measurements. Four-foot-high drifts. Almost as tall as Zeke. And then he uttered the words that Zeke had been waiting for.

"This is the blizzard of the decade!"

"Oh, no," Mom said.

Zeke pumped his fist in the air. "Oh, yes!"

15

The Calm after the Storm

Friday morning

By morning, the blizzard had blown through. The sky was blue, and the winds light. No more howling. Freeze Jones was right. The blizzard was a giant storm, but it had moved fast.

Mom said, "It's the calm after the storm." She dipped bread in egg for the French toast.

She was still wearing her earmuffs.

Zeke turned on the radio. "All schools in Green River are delayed for three hours," the announcer said.

"That's good," said Mom. "It's still dangerous out there."

"Yay!" shouted Bub. "We can have a snowball fight, Zeke!"

"No, thanks."

Today was the deadline for the contest. He still hadn't taken his winter photo. Zeke needed a whole snow day, not a three-hour delay.

Mom brought over the French toast, but Zeke only ate three slices instead of his usual six.

If only he could talk to Dad! Zeke got up from the table and called Dad's satellite phone. A recording came on saying that all communication was down due to bad weather. Zeke shut his eyes and heard Dad's voice in his head. Dad always told him, *I have faith in you, kiddo. Go get 'em.*

Zeke grabbed Storm Shooter and Sky Tracker from the counter. He had to get busy. First, he'd record his weather readings. Then he'd snap photos of snowdrifts.

When he opened the back door, a blast of cold air hit his face.

"Wait one minute!" Mom called behind him.

She took off her earmuffs. "Put them on," she said. "And don't forget to put on your snow pants."

Outside, Zeke took one step and sank into a huge drift of snow. Getting out of it took forever. He used a shovel to make a path.

His weather station was buried under another giant drift. He swept the snow away with the shovel.

What a disaster! The thermometer had cracked. Kiho's weather vane had toppled over. The barometer was gone. It must have blown away. Zeke couldn't take any measurements. His Mood Meter sank to 100 degrees below zero.

At least he could take his winter photo. But when he aimed Storm Shooter at a drift, all he saw was a white blob. What he needed was an amazing icicle or ...

"Hey, Zeke the Weather Geek! Wanna make a snowperson?"

Kiho and Luna climbed over the snowdrift by the garage. Luna's purple boots stood out in the whiteness.

Kiho brought the skis he made last winter. "Where's your scooter?"

"I can't use my scooter in the snow."

But Kiho had his tool kit. After shoveling a path to the shed, they pushed the door open. Then they dragged the scooter from the shed. Kiho quickly removed the wheels and added the skis in their place.

Zeke tested it out on the path. He slid a little, but the skis worked!

Luna and Kiho started to make a snowperson, but the snow was too dry to stick together. They gave up.

"Isn't it a little late to take your winter photo?" asked Luna, pointing at his camera.

Zeke's Mood Meter hit rock bottom. Nothing was going right. His weather station was destroyed. He couldn't talk to Dad. All Zeke's contest photos were duds. And now Luna was rubbing it in.

Kiho patted Zeke on the shoulder and said, "Let me look at your shots."

He scrolled through the photos. Then he stopped.

"That's it!" Kiho tapped the screen. "That's the one."

"Let me see!" Luna said.

Zeke shut his camera screen off before Luna could make fun of it.

Kiho gave Zeke a high-five. "It's a winner, Zeke the Weather Geek!"

He hoped Kiho was right. But he could just hear Luna saying, "Where's the snow?" What if the photo didn't even qualify for the contest?

Mrs. Gully, Zeke's neighbor, came over with Lady, her Chihuahua.

"Can I borrow your camera?" Kiho asked. "I can't believe it's taken me this long to find a picture."

"No problem, bro," Zeke replied.

Kiho snapped a picture of the tiny dog against a huge snowdrift. The boys both had their photos.

"Come inside, kids, for some cocoa!" Mom yelled out the door.

Luna drank her cocoa quickly. "Thanks, Mrs. Abramovich. I have to get to school now to help Miss Li."

Zeke scowled. Of course, she's helping Miss Li!

After they finished their cocoa, Zeke and Kiho printed out their photos in Mom's office.

Brring. Brring. Brring.

Mom's cell phone was ringing on her desk. "Can you get that, Zeke?" she called from the kitchen.

It was Dad calling from Antarctica!

"How's the blizzard?" Dad said. "I heard all about it on my radio. And how's the lizard? Lizards aren't like penguins. They are cold —"

"I know!" shouted Zeke. "Cold-blooded animals. They can't drink cocoa to warm up! I kept her warm with the Polar Penguin Project fleece you sent me."

"That's great!" Dad shouted back. "About the dog ..."

The line started to sputter. Zeke had almost forgotten about wanting a Saint Bernard. He wanted to tell Dad about the blizzard and more about the lizard. But the phone went dead.

Zeke missed Dad more than ever. He climbed upstairs to see the lizard. He leaned over the tank and showed her his photo. She nibbled the corner.

Bub was on his bed, reading a dinosaur book. He put down the book.

"She likes it," Bub said. "And I think she likes you."

Meteorology

✳ Meteorology is not the study of meteors and meteorites!

✳ It's the scientific study of Earth's atmosphere, with a focus on weather forecasting.

✳ The word *meteorology* comes from the Greek words *meteoros*, meaning "things in the air" and *logos*, meaning "the study of."

✳ Weather is affected by six major elements in the atmosphere: wind, temperature, humidity, precipitation, air pressure and cloudiness.

✳ Meteorology is the science of how these six elements interact and change over time, making different kinds of weather.

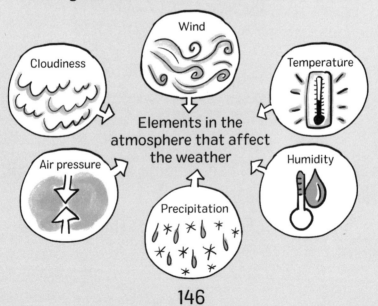

Cloudiness

Wind

Temperature

Air pressure

Elements in the atmosphere that affect the weather

Humidity

Precipitation

What Is a Meteorologist?

* Meteorologists are expert weather watchers.

* They use science and math to observe, analyze and forecast the weather.

* They collect information from satellites, radar and weather stations around the world.

* With the help of computer models and scientific principles, meteorologists make short- and long-term weather forecasts.

* They also track atmospheric patterns and climate conditions around the globe.

* Meteorologists focus on the troposphere, the layer of the atmosphere closest to Earth where weather happens.

Troposphere

Troposphere

By the way, a scientist who studies meteors and meteorites is a meteoriticist. That's an awesome job, too!

Famous Meteorologists

Aristotle was a philosopher and scientist in ancient Greece. He wrote about the weather and other earth sciences in his work *Meteorologica* around 340 BCE. He was curious about clouds, wind, lightning and other things in the atmosphere, and his work helped start the science of meteorology.

June Bacon-Bercey was the first female TV meteorologist. She went on the air for WGR-TV in Buffalo, New York, in 1972. She went on to be a meteorologist for the National Weather Service and the National Oceanic and Atmospheric Administration. She was also the first Black woman in the United States to earn a degree in meteorology from the University of California, Los Angeles. With money won on a TV quiz show, Bacon-Bercey started a fund for young women studying atmospheric sciences.

Zeke Abramovich became interested in weather when he noticed a pattern: his hair was frizziest on humid and rainy days. Zeke decided to learn how to forecast weather. That way, he would know when he was about to get the frizzies.

Winter Photo Contest

Friday afternoon

"Where's the snow?"

Luna was pointing at Zeke's photo. It was the only one without snow in it.

Miss Li had hung the students' winter photos around the room. There was Luna's picture of the first snowflake, Kiho's of Lady, the Chihuahua, Simon's of the salt truck and lots of photos of the blizzard. Luna was right. Zeke's was the only one that didn't have snow.

In Zeke's photo, the lizard was curled on his chest during the blackout.

"It's not a winter photo!" Luna stomped away in her purple boots.

"Zeke took the picture of his lizard during the blizzard," Miss Li told the class.

"It's totally cool," Kiho whispered to Zeke.

Miss Li told everyone to get in their seats. "A three-hour delay means we have to catch up on a whole morning's worth of work."

Why wasn't she talking about the blizzard of the decade? Miss Li always had to get in her spelling and math. Go figure.

Zeke couldn't concentrate. He fidgeted and doodled until, finally, Miss Li said, "I bet you're all wondering about the Winter Photo Contest."

Duh! There wasn't much time left. It was 1:45, and school ended at 2:30. Suddenly the classroom door opened.

Zeke stared in disbelief. Was he imagining it? He blinked again. No, it was definitely him. Freeze Jones. The Weather Warrior himself was actually walking into their classroom!

He was dressed from head to toe in his

blizzard outfit. Weather gadgets hung from every pocket.

"Welcome, Mr. Freeze Jones!" Miss Li said. "Class, give our favorite weather forecaster a round of applause. He's going to judge the contest entries."

Zeke clapped the loudest.

"Thank you, students. I hope you all stayed safe and toasty warm during the blizzard," he said in his booming voice. "By the way, I got my start in meteorology when I won the Winter Photo Contest right in this room. And now, here I am at WXYZ-TV."

Zeke sat up straighter. He didn't know that's how Freeze Jones got his start on being a Weather Warrior. Now Zeke had even more reason to want to win the contest.

Freeze Jones cleared his throat. "Give me a few minutes to look at your winter photos."

Slowly he walked around the room, examining all the photos. He stopped in front of each one. Peered at it. Took a few notes on his notepad. And then moved on.

Finally, he returned to the front of the room. He cleared his throat and wiggled the knot on his snowflake bow tie.

"I am ready to announce the winners. Third place goes to Simon Evans for 'The Salt Truck.' Second place goes to Luna Díaz for her 'First Snowflake.' And the winner is ... Zeke Abramovich for 'Lizard Rescue.'"

Then he read the caption aloud. "'There's a lizard in my blizzard: Boy rescues lizard from blizzard blackout.'"

Everyone clapped and cheered. Zeke glowed so brightly he felt like he could melt the biggest snowdrift in Green River. His Mood Meter shot through the roof.

Freeze Jones continued his speech. "Lizards are very sensitive to cold and heat. This photo captures the dangers and wonders of winter."

The lizard was a weather instrument! A true weather geek like Zeke. She had taught him that the weather was all around them. It was even in his own house. Saint Bernards weren't the only pets for a weather geek.

"Zeke rocks!" Kiho exclaimed.

Miss Li asked the three winners to come up for their awards. They each got a scroll tied with a gold ribbon. Zeke unrolled his scroll.

And then Freeze Jones handed him a small package. Inside was a real barometer. His homemade one had blown away in the storm. Now he could set up his weather station again.

"You're a hero, Zeke Abramovich," Freeze Jones said. "Saving your lizard makes you a real Weather Warrior."

Was this really happening to him? Or was it just a dream?

Oh, it was real. Kiho nudged him. Luna tossed her purple hair and flashed a tiny smile. Zeke expected her to say that she deserved first place. She never lost a contest! Remarkably, she didn't say a thing.

"Keep your eyes on the skies, Zeke," Freeze Jones boomed. Then he gave Zeke a high five.

Zeke high-fived him back. "You bet I will, sir."

158

"By the way, what's your lizard's name?" Freeze Jones asked.

Zeke thought for a minute. He remembered the name for his Saint Bernard puppy. He took a deep breath.

"Blizzard."

Freeze Jones smiled. "I like that. Now, back to the weather! You better take care out there! The temperature is dropping. We're in for a deep freeze."

No problem. Zeke had his lucky new barometer. Maybe he'd nickname it Lucky. But before he could rebuild his weather station, he had to stop off at Stan the Snake Man's Amazing Pet Store. With the roads cleared, the cricket shipment might have come in. On a special day like this one, Blizzard deserved an extra-special supper.

Keeping a Weather Journal

Zeke's Sky Tracker helps him to observe the weather and make forecasts. He couldn't be a weather geek without his weather journal! Want to keep one, too? Here are some tips.

* At the same time every day, observe what's happening with the weather.

* Use your senses. Is it hot or cold? Wet or dry? Windy or calm? Cloudy or clear?

* If you have weather instruments, take readings of:

Blizzard is a weather geek like me!

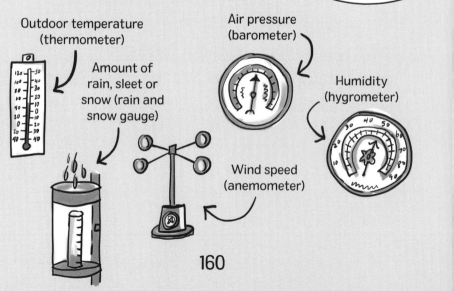

Outdoor temperature (thermometer)

Amount of rain, sleet or snow (rain and snow gauge)

Air pressure (barometer)

Humidity (hygrometer)

Wind speed (anemometer)

* When a storm is coming, you might want to take readings more often.
* Note how much of the sky is covered in clouds.
* Record the information in your journal.
* Look for patterns. Be on your toes when the wind blows. The weather may be changing!
* Try writing a forecast for the next day.
* Remember, your eyes are important tools for weather watching!

Hint:
Symbols can be a quick way to record weather information.

Sun   Rain   Windy   Cloudy   Lightning   Snow

Hint:
Take pictures. Record that amazing icicle or snowdrift before it melts! Photographs can help you track weather changes from day to day.

Click!

SKY TRACKER

Date: Wednesday, December 5
Time: 3:45 p.m.

General Weather Conditions

Temperature: 17 degrees Fahrenheit

Barometric Pressure: Falling super fast!!!

Precipitation: Snow: 2 inches

Wind Speed: 23 miles per hour

Wind Direction: Northeast

Humidity: Humid!

Hair frizzy!!

YES!!!

Almost a blizzard!

163

Zeke's Weather Words

air mass: a large body of air, moving moisture and heat through the atmosphere

air pressure or barometric pressure: force exerted by the weight of air in the atmosphere pressing down on Earth

astronomy: scientific study of stars, planets and other objects in outer space

atmosphere: layer of gases, including oxygen and carbon dioxide, that surround Earth

barometer: instrument that measures air pressure

blizzard: huge snowstorm with very strong winds that lasts three hours or longer

Blizzard Warning: U.S. National Weather Service announcement issued when blizzard conditions are expected or occurring, advising people to stay safe

Celsius: temperature scale in which water freezes at 0 degrees

climate: general weather conditions in a region over a long period of time

climate change: change in average conditions such as temperature and rainfall in a region over a long period of time

Fahrenheit: temperature scale in which water freezes at 32 degrees above zero

humidity: amount of water vapor in the air

meteorologist: scientist who studies and predicts the weather

meteorology: study of the atmosphere, including weather and how to forecast it

snow: tiny ice crystals that form from water vapor in the air

thermometer: instrument that measures temperature

water vapor: water in the form of a gas

weather: state of the atmosphere at a particular time and place: clear or cloudy, for example

Winter Storm Watch: advisory issued when there's a possibility of dangerous winter weather within 48 hours

wintry mix: mixture of rain, freezing rain, sleet or snow

SELECTED SOURCES

BOOKS

Breen, Mark, and Kathleen Friestad. *The Kids' Book of Weather Forecasting.* Tennessee: Worthy Publishing, 2008.

Farndon, John, Sean Callery, and Miranda Smith. *Weather.* New York: Scholastic, Inc., 2020.

Murphy, Jim. *Blizzard!* New York: Scholastic Press, 2000.

Rupp, Rebecca. *Weather!* Massachusetts: Storey Publishing LLC, 2003.

WEBSITES

"Blizzards." University Corporation for Atmospheric Research (UCAR) Center for Science Education. 2019. https://scied.ucar.edu/learning-zone/storms/blizzards

"Climate Basics for Kids." Center for Climate and Energy Solutions (C2ES). https://www.c2es.org/content/climate-basics-for-kids/

Climate.gov. National Oceanic and Atmospheric Administration (NOAA). March 15, 2021. https://www.climate.gov

"How Weather Works." University Corporation for Atmospheric Research (UCAR) Center for Science Education. 2021. https://scied.ucar.edu/learning-zone/how-weather-works

Kornei, Katherine. "June Bacon-Bercey: Pioneering Meteorologist and Passionate Supporter of Science." Eos. February 17, 2020. https://eos.org/features/june-bacon-bercey-pioneering-meteorologist-and-passionate-supporter-of-science

Means, Tiffany. "What is Meteorology?" ThoughtCo. August 25, 2020. https://www.thoughtco.com/what-is-meteorology-3444439

National Weather Service. National Oceanic and Aeronautics Administration (NOAA). https://www.weather.gov

"Severe Weather 101 — Winter Weather." National Severe Storms Laboratory/National Oceanic and Atmospheric Administration (NOAA). https://www.nssl.noaa.gov/education/svrwx101/winter/types/

"Water and Ice: How Do Snowflakes Form?" SciJinks, National Oceanic and Atmospheric Association. November 28, 2021. https://scijinks.gov/snowflakes/

Joan Axelrod-Contrada writes fiction and nonfiction for children and young adults. The author of over 20 books for young people, she is also a journalist and writing teacher, and has an MFA in Writing for Children and Young Adults from Vermont College of Fine Arts. Growing up in the Boston area, Joan watched TV meteorologists every night, and she credits them with cultivating her love of the weather. Joan lives in Northampton, Massachusetts.

Ann Malaspina has written over 30 books for young people about the environment, social issues and human rights. A former journalist, Ann has an MFA in Writing for Children and Young Adults from Vermont College of Fine Arts. Ann's interest in the weather blossomed after she joined the community garden near her home in Ridgewood, New Jersey.

Paula J. Becker has illustrated more than 30 books for children, and her fun, whimsical work has been published in many children's magazines. Born and raised in South Texas, Paula rarely saw more than a flake or two of snow. Today at her home in Pointe Claire, Quebec, Paula has become very familiar with snow, and shovels a lot of it!